The Feathered Crown

Marsha Hayles

ILLUSTRATED BY Bernadette Pons

HENRY HOLT AND COMPANY ▪ NEW YORK

To my sisters,
Mary and Marj,
who have always helped me to fly
—M. H.

To my little Emma
—B. P.

Henry Holt and Company, LLC, *Publishers since 1866*, 115 West 18th Street, New York, New York 10011
(www.henryholt.com) Henry Holt is a registered trademark of Henry Holt and Company, LLC
Text copyright © 2002 by Marsha Hayles. Illustrations copyright © 2002 by Bernadette Pons
All rights reserved. Distributed in Canada by H. B. Fenn and Company Ltd.
Library of Congress Cataloging-in-Publication Data
Hayles, Marsha. The feathered crown / by Marsha Hayles; illustrated by Bernadette Pons.
Summary: Mother birds take a long journey to welcome the newborn baby Jesus and give him a feathered
crown to warm his head. 1. Jesus Christ—Nativity—Juvenile fiction. [1. Jesus Christ—Nativity—Fiction.
2. Birds—Fiction. 3. Stories in rhyme.] I. Pons, Bernadette, ill. II. Title. PZ8.3.H326 Fe 2002 [E]—dc21
2001006737 / ISBN 0-8050-6421-4 / First Edition—2002 / Designed by Donna Mark
Printed in the United States of America on acid-free paper. ∞ 10 9 8 7 6 5 4 3 2 1

The artist used watercolor on Lanaquarelle paper to create the illustrations for this book.

The mother birds,
Like gentle words,
Took wing one wintry day.

In subtle browns
And gray-soft down,
They rose to find their way.

Across the plains
With stubbled grains
And hills with whispered snow,
They took their flight
Into the night,
A world away to go.

At each stop
The muted flock
Took others to the fold.

They journeyed on
From field to pond
In clouds of graying cold,

Beyond the trees,
Then out to sea
Aloft on heaven's breath—

Wave over wave,
Day after day,
Wingward on their quest.

At last warm land,
A sea of sand,
The mothers touched the earth—

A place so strange,
So soon to change,
Awaiting one child's birth.

They gathered bits
Of straw and sticks,
And leaves to cushion best—

To build a home,
A manger throne,
A feather-softened nest.

Then soon another
Weary mother,
With baby swaddled tight,
Saw the nest
And knew that rest
Would bless her child that night.

She thanked the birds
With gentle words
And put her Son to bed.
A feathered crown
Of humble down
Soon warmed the new King's head.

So on that night
Though tired by flight
The mothers did their part.

Their journey done,
New life begun—
A gift from heaven's heart.